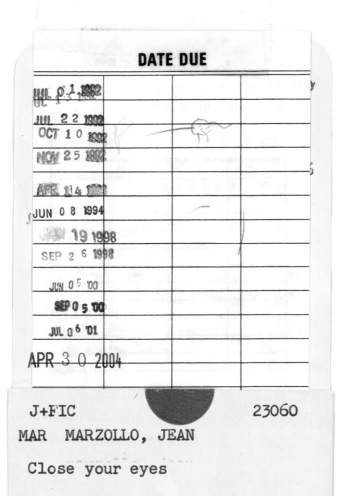

Close Your Eyes

Jean Marzollo
Close Your Eyes
pictures by Susan Jeffers

The Dial Press
New York

a pied piper book

CLOSE YOUR EYES
is published in a hardcover edition by The Dial Press,
1 Dag Hammarskjold Plaza, New York, New York 10017.
ISBN 0-8037-1617-6

for David Andre Bates Marzollo
for Little Ernie

Close your eyes and you can be

Sound asleep in an apple tree

Or if you like

on a ship at sea.

Close your eyes and you can play

With woolly lambs on a lazy day

Or tabby cats in a pile of hay.

Close your eyes and you can lie

Hidden deep in a field of rye

Or on a cloud in a sunset sky.

Close your eyes and gently rest

Cuddled on a panda's chest

Or with a friend in a robin's nest.

Close your eyes and with a yawn

Imagine drowsy geese at dawn

Or lightning bugs on a quiet lawn.

But you've not heard a word I've said

For you're asleep in a cozy bed

With secret dreams in your lovely head.

Goodnight.